Miss Lily's FABULOUS Pink Feather Boa

MARGARET WILD
KERRY ARGENT

PUFFIN BOOKS

Potoroos are small mammals found in different parts of Australia. The Broad-faced Potoroo is extinct, the Long-footed Potoroo, on which the Last Potoroo is based, is a rare and little-known species, and the population of the Long-nosed Potoroo varies considerably, depending on the area.

PUFFIN BOOKS

Published by the Penguin Group
Penguin Group (Australia)
250 Camberwell Road, Camberwell, Victoria 3124, Australia
(a division of Pearson Australia Group Pty Ltd)
Penguin Group (USA) Inc.
375 Hudson Street, New York, New York 10014, USA
Penguin Group (Canada)
10 Alcorn Avenue, Toronto, Ontario, Canada M4V 3B2
(a division of Pearson Penguin Canada Inc.)
Penguin Books Ltd
80 Strand, London WC2R 0RL, England
Penguin Ireland
25 St Stephen's Green, Dublin 2, Ireland
(a division of Penguin Books Ltd)
Penguin Books India Pvt Ltd
11, Community Centre, Panchsheel Park, New Delhi-110 017, India
Penguin Group (NZ)
Cnr Airborne and Rosedale Roads, Albany, Auckland, New Zealand
(a division of Pearson New Zealand Ltd)
Penguin Books (South Africa) (Pty) Ltd
24 Sturdee Avenue, Rosebank, Johannesburg 2196, South Africa

Penguin Books Ltd, Registered Offices: 80 Strand, London WC2R 0RL, England

First published by Penguin Books Australia, 1998
Published in Puffin, 1999

9 11 13 15 17 19 20 18 16 14 12 10

Copyright © Margaret Wild, 1998
Illustrations copyright © Kerry Argent, 1998

The moral right of the author and illustrator has been asserted

Designed by Cathy Larsen, Penguin Design Studio
Text designed by Kerry Argent
Typeset in Cochin
Made and printed in China by Everbest Printing Co. Ltd.

National Library of Australia
Cataloguing-in-Publication data:

Wild, Margaret, 1948– .
Miss Lily's fabulous pink feather boa.
ISBN 0 14 055902 7
1. Endangered animals – Australia – Juvenile fiction.
2. Potorous tridactylus – Juvenile fiction. I. Argent, Kerry, 1960– . II. Title.

A823.3

Illustrator's technique: watercolour

www.puffin.com.au

U P NORTH, where the hibiscus flowers were as big as dinner plates and the trees blossomed with white cockatoos, was Miss Lily's Tropical Holiday House.

When the Last Potoroo struggled up the steps of the holiday house with her big suitcase, she nearly died of fright.

She'd had no idea that Miss Lily was a crocodile,

*and such a **BIG** one!*

During dinner, the Last Potoroo kept glancing nervously at Miss Lily's enormous snout, at her strong, sharp teeth.

She felt much better when Miss Lily said kindly, 'I have a very small appetite and I only eat fish.'

Later that night, when the other guests went up to bed, Miss Lily asked the Last Potoroo to have a cup of peppermint tea with her on the veranda.

At first the Last Potoroo was too shy to say much, but she soon found herself confessing, 'I'm so lonely. I think I'm the only Potoroo left in the whole of Australia.'

Miss Lily patted her paw. 'I'm sure that somewhere there are others of your kind,' she said. 'You must be brave. You must go looking for them.'

'Maybe – one day,' said the Last Potoroo. But she didn't know if she'd ever be brave enough to journey very far.

During the day, the guests rowed down
the long brown river, went for walks in
the rainforest, and lazed in the hammocks.
Sometimes the Last Potoroo joined them,
but mostly she just followed Miss Lily around,
or sat for hours on top of the hill, gazing at
the long red road that wound south.

In the evenings,
Miss Lily took off her
apron, put on a fabulous
pink feather boa – and
danced the tango. The boa,
which had belonged to
Miss Lily's mother and,
before that, to her mother's
mother, made Miss Lily
look splendid. So young,
so carefree, so joyful!

When Miss Lily finished dancing, she always flung her feather boa into the crowd. Once, the Last Potoroo caught it, and as she draped it around herself, everyone exclaimed: 'It suits you. You look wonderful!'

The Last Potoroo sparkled, feeling for a moment that she could do anything – and everything!

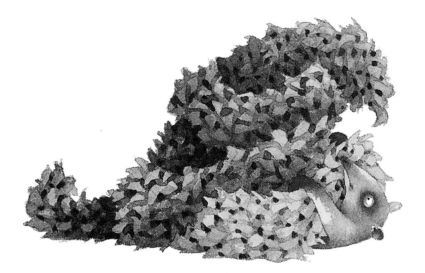

It seemed to the Last Potoroo that the feather boa was somehow magical. She started dreaming about it, and when she woke up in the mornings, she longed for the evenings, so that she could once more see the boa – and if she was lucky, catch it and drape it around herself.

One morning, while Miss Lily was weeding the vegetable garden, the Last Potoroo tiptoed into Miss Lily's bedroom, and opened the trunk in which the feather boa was kept. She only wanted to put it on for a moment, just to feel it curling around her. But, as if in a trance, she found herself picking up a pair of scissors from Miss Lily's dressing-table – *and snipping off a piece of the boa.*

Humming under
her breath, the Last
Potoroo folded the
feather boa away in
the trunk, and took
the little piece to her
own room.

She slept for a while, but when she woke up and saw the scrap of boa next to her on the pillow, she was horrified. How could she have done such a thing? *And what would Miss Lily say when she found out?*

But the next time Miss Lily wore the fabulous pink feather boa she didn't seem to notice anything different about it.

The Last Potoroo buried
the piece of boa at the bottom
of the hill. For nights afterwards,
she was plagued with dreams
of the boa wriggling out of the
soil and dancing up the steps
of the holiday house.

At the end of the month, the guests went
home, family after family, until only the
Last Potoroo was left.

'Goodbye,' said Miss Lily.

'Goodbye,' said the Last Potoroo, struggling
down the steps with her big suitcase. She
didn't want to go home. She wished she could
stay longer, perhaps as Miss Lily's helper.

'Wait!' said Miss Lily.

The Last Potoroo turned around, beaming.

'This is for you,' said Miss Lily, and she gave the Last Potoroo her fabulous pink feather boa.

'Oh!' said the Last Potoroo. 'Thank you!' She wrapped the boa around her body – around, and around, and around. As she did so, her eyes shone, her fur was gleaming, and she felt that she could do anything – and everything!

Suddenly her joy evaporated. 'I can't take this,' she whispered. 'I did something dreadful. I wanted the boa so much that I stole a bit of it.'

'I know,' said Miss Lily softly.

They hugged each other, hard.

'I hope she finds what she's looking for,' said Miss Lily, as she watched the Last Potoroo disappear along the red road that wound south.

I N THE MONTHS that followed, Miss Lily
often thought about the Last Potoroo.
One afternoon she received a postcard.

It said:

Dear Miss Lily,
I can't wait to tell
you my news!
See you next Sunday—
and please make a
booking for ten!
Your good friend
No-Longer-the-Last
Potoroo

45¢

~ POTOROO DOWNS ~
5.9.97

Miss Lily
C/- Miss Lily's Tropical
Holiday House

And taped to the postcard were two tiny
pink feathers.

Very early the next Sunday,
No-Longer-the-Last Potoroo and her new friends
tiptoed through the gate of the Holiday House
and up the steps to surprise Miss Lily –

with the biggest hug ever!